A Kalmus Classic Edition

Johann Sebastian
BACH

CONCERTO IN D MINOR

FOR TWO PIANOS/FOUR HANDS

K 03029

CONCERTO.

Johann Sebastian Bach.

I
I
cresc.
cresc.
f
mf
B
B
p
I
I

cresc.
dolce
C
C.

Solo.
p
p non legato
cresc.
f
f
p
p
E
E

cresc.
f
dimin.   poco a poco
f
dimin.   poco a poco
non legato
p
p

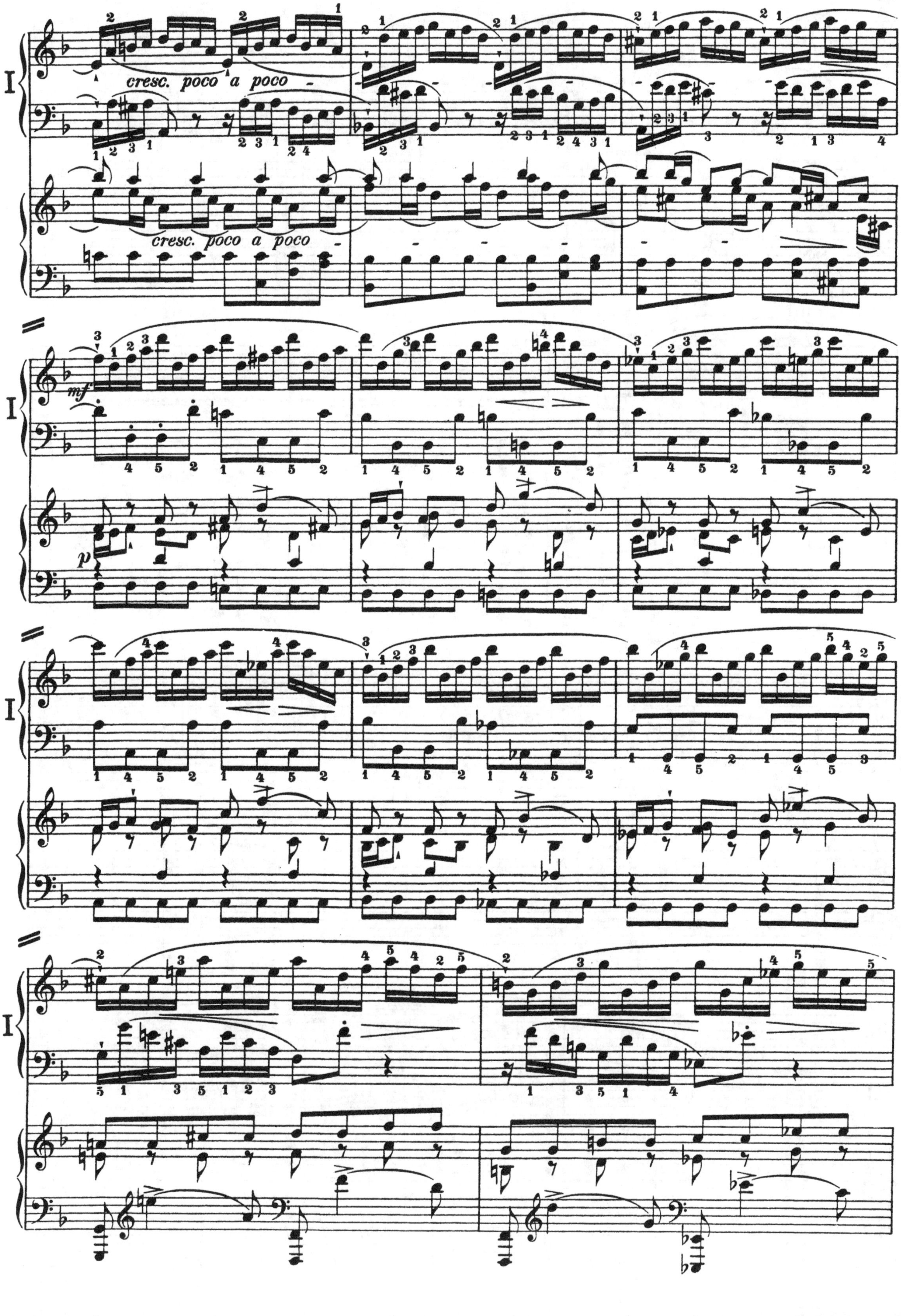
I
cresc. poco a poco
cresc. poco a poco
I
mf
p
I
I

Tutti.
Solo.
mf
f
f
p
ptr
R.
L.
R.
L.
f
f
R.
L.
p
cresc.
p
cresc.

di - mi - nu - en - do poco
a poco
p
pp
K
K
I
I
I
I

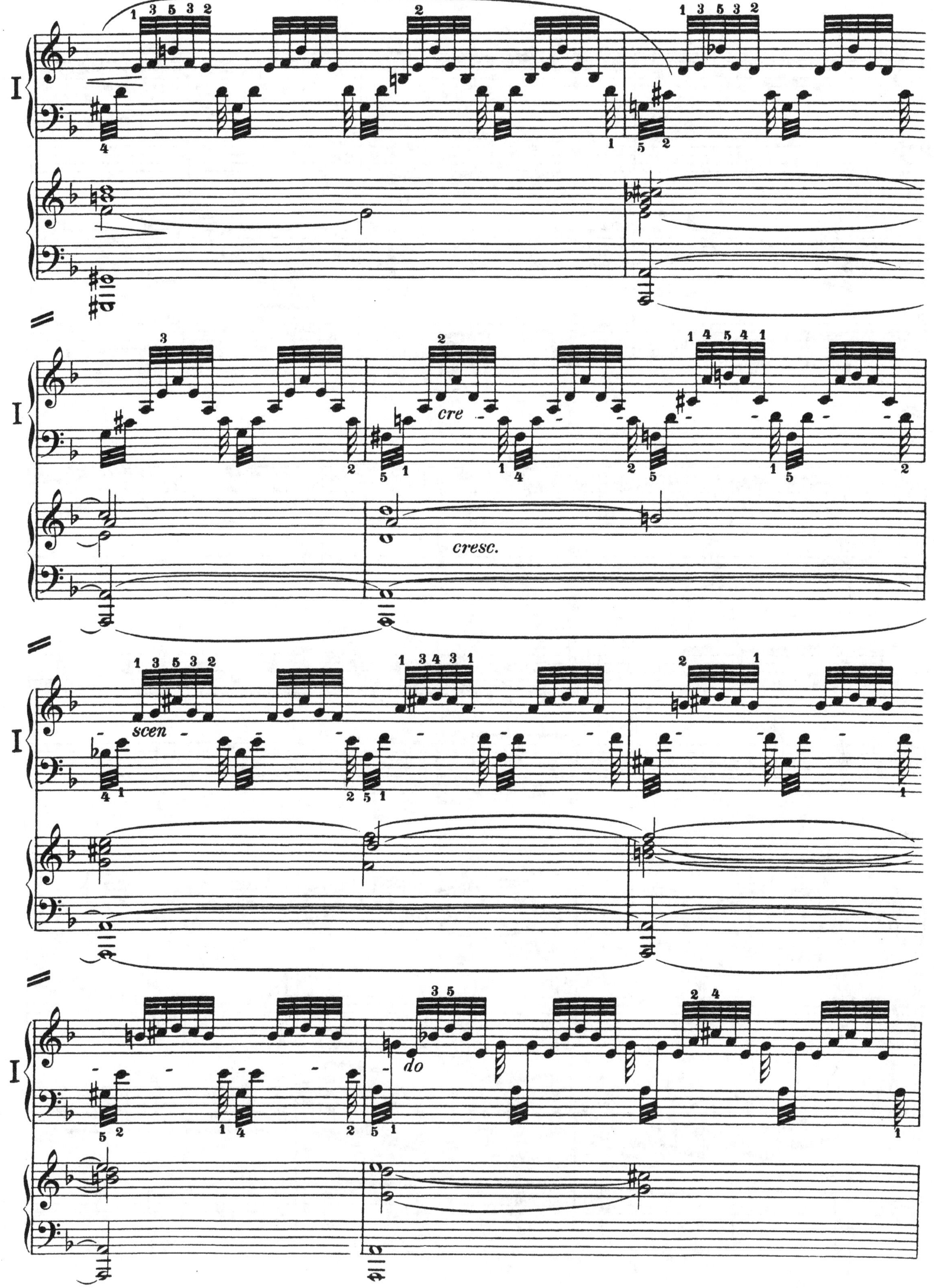
cre
cresc.
scen
do

L
Tutti.
Solo.
f
p
p
L
p
cresc. poco
mf
cresc. poco
mf
L.

Adagio. (♪ = 96.)
Adagio. (♪ = 96.)
A espress.
A
cresc.
poco cresc.
tr.

dimin.
p
cresc.
mf
f
f
f
f
E
E

Allegro moderato. (♩ = 96.)
mf
cresc.
Allegro moderato. (♩ = 96.)
mf
cresc.
f
f
Solo.
f
mf
f
mf

I
mf
f
mf
mf
f
f
p
I
cresc. poco-
cresc. poco-
B
f
p
B
f
p
f
I
f
mf
Tutti.
cresc.-
mf
mf
cresc.-

Tutti.
Solo.
mf
f
mf
C
f
p
C
f
p
cresc.
cresc.
dim.
mf
f
p
dim.
mf
f
p
I
I
I
I

Solo.
mf
mf
cresc.
cresc.
f
f
mf

Solo.
mf
f
mf
f
Tutti
G
Solo.
mf
p
mf
p
mf
p
mf
p

p
R.
L.
dimin.

I
p cresc. f
H
I
f mf
H
mf
I
f mf
I
cresc. f

Tutti
Solo.
sf
sf
f
dim.
mf
mf
cresc.
f
mf
cresc.
f
mf

ritard. poco
Adagio.
Tutti.
a tempo
cresc.
Adagio.
a tempo
cresc.
f
mf
ritard.
Fine.
ritard.
Fine.